CLASSIC STARTS™

The Prince and the Pauper

Retold from the Mark Twain original
by Kathleen Olmstead

Illustrated by Jamel Akib

Sterling Publishing Co., Inc.
New York

Library of Congress Cataloging-in-Publication Data

Olmstead, Kathleen.
  The prince and the pauper / retold from the Mark Twain original by
Kathleen Olmstead ; illustrated by Jamel Akib ; afterword by Arthur Pober.
    p. cm.——(Classic starts)
Summary: An abridged version of the Mark Twain classic in which young
Edward VI of England and a poor boy who resembles him exchange places and
each learns something about the other's very different station in life.
  ISBN-13: 978-1-4027-3687-2
  ISBN-10: 1-4027-3687-8
1. Edward VI, King of England, 1537–1553—Juvenile fiction. [1. Edward VI,
King of England, 1537–1553—Fiction. 2. Mistaken identity—Fiction.
3. Adventure and adventurers—Fiction. 4. Great Britain—History—Edward VI,
1547–1553—Fiction.] I. Akib, Jamel, ill. II. Twain, Mark, 1835–1910. Prince and
the pauper. III. Title. IV. Series.

PZ7.O499Pri 2007
[Fic]—dc22

                                                    2006014803

                    2 4 6 8 10 9 7 5 3 1

                   Published by Sterling Publishing Co., Inc.
                   387 Park Avenue South, New York, NY 10016
                     Copyright © 2007 by Kathleen Olmstead
                    Illustrations copyright © 2007 by Jamel Akib
                   Distributed in Canada by Sterling Publishing
                    ^c/_o Canadian Manda Group, 165 Dufferin Street,
                        Toronto, Ontario, Canada M6K 3H6
          Distributed in the United Kingdom by GMC Distribution Services,
          Castle Place, 166 High Street, Lewes, East Sussex, England BN7 1XU
             Distributed in Australia by Capricorn Link (Australia) Pty. Ltd.
                      P.O. Box 704, Windsor, NSW 2756, Australia

             Classic Starts is a trademark of Sterling Publishing Co., Inc.

                  Sterling ISBN-13: 978-1-4027-3687-2
                      ISBN-10: 1-4027-3687-8

        For information about custom editions, special sales, premium and
           corporate purchases, please contact Sterling Special Sales
         Department at 800-805-5489 or specialsales@sterlingpub.com.

CONTENTS

❧

CHAPTER 1

The Births of the Prince and the Pauper

⌒

A great many years ago, a baby boy was born in the city of London. His name was Tom Canty. His family was very poor and could not afford him. On the same day, in a different part of London, a baby boy was born to a rich family who wanted him very much. His name was Edward Tudor and his father was the king of England.

As a matter of fact, all of England wanted this little boy. People cheered in the streets when he was born. Strangers hugged each other and wept tears of joy. There was music and dancing, parties and parades. Everyone—especially King Henry—wished for a boy. Although he had two older sisters, Edward was now heir to the throne. One day he would be the king.

Edward, Prince of Wales, paid no attention to all the fuss. He slept wrapped in silks in his warm bed. He didn't have a care in the world. The king and queen, lords and ladies of the court, and important politicians all watched over him.

Young Tom Canty did not have the same restful sleep. He slept wrapped in rags. There was no wood for his fire. His mother worried how she would find the money to feed this new child. She loved Tom dearly and was happy to have him, but she feared life would be hard for the poor little babe. She could barely afford food for her other children. Mrs. Canty kissed Tom's forehead and wished him pleasant dreams.

Several years passed. Edward was surrounded

by riches and jewels, while Tom had very little to call his own. Nevertheless, they both grew into strong, helpful, and smart boys.

Tom Canty and his family lived close to the London Bridge on a street called Offal Court. Their building was old and close to falling down. Tom lived on the third floor with his parents, grandmother, and older twin sisters, Nan and Bet. They all lived in one room. Tom's parents had a bed tucked into a corner of the room. His grandmother slept in the opposite corner. Tom and his sisters had more freedom with their sleeping arrangements. They could choose to sleep anywhere on the floor that they liked.

Nan and Bet were fifteen years old. The girls were caring, good-hearted people, just like their mother. Mr. Canty and their grandmother, on the other hand, were not so kind. He was a thief, and she earned her money by begging in the street.

Mr. Canty had tried to turn his children into thieves, but Nan, Bet, and Tom would not steal. And so the children had to beg. If they did not bring home enough money, Mr. Canty became very angry. Sometimes he yelled at them—especially Tom—in moments of rage.

Tom's father often sent him to bed without supper. "If you can't bring money into the house, then you get nothing to eat," Mr. Canty said. On those nights, Tom's mother would sneak him food—a tiny scrap or morsel that she had saved from her own meal. Everyone felt hungry in the Canty household. There was never enough food to go around.

Yet despite his many hardships, young Tom was happy with his life. It was the same as that of all of his friends. He didn't know there was any other way to live.

One day an old priest named Father Andrew

moved into the building. He did not have a parish of his own anymore, so he lived among the poor. The priest often took time out of his day to teach the Canty children how to read and write. Mr. Canty thought that spending time with books meant less time begging in the streets, so the children had to learn in secret. Tom was a very interested student. He loved the world of books and reading. The old priest even taught him a few words of Latin.

Tom began to spend more and more time in his "school." The priest told him tales of knights and giants, fairies, enchanted castles, kings, and princes. Soon Tom's head was full of these stories. He lay awake at night and let his imagination run away with him. He tried to forget all about the straw mat he lay on and his empty belly. Instead he thought about life inside the castle walls. Over time, Tom developed one very strong wish. He wanted to see a real live prince.

As Tom read more about the elegant lives of kings and princes, he began to notice how shabby his own clothes were. He came to realize that not everyone went to bed hungry each night. There were some people who did not have to beg on the streets for small scraps of food. He still played with his friends and enjoyed himself, but something had changed. While he used to enjoy playing in the mud and water of the river Thames, Tom now used this time to wash and clean himself. He was slowly trying to change. He wanted to be more like the people in the stories Father Andrew told him.

When he was alone with his friends, Tom organized a royal court and appointed himself prince. He told everyone how they should act and what they should do. His friends enjoyed the game, so they played along. No one realized that

Tom considered their play to be more than that. He was practicing for the day when he might actually be at court.

Despite these fun moments, Tom still spent the better part of his day in his rags, begging on the streets. He still went home each night knowing that his father and grandmother might take their anger out on him. He still had to wait for his mother to sneak food to him late at night. Through all of this, his desire to see a real prince grew stronger.

One January day, Tom walked through the streets sad and barefoot. There was a cold rain and Tom did not have a coat or umbrella. He looked into shop windows at sandwiches, soup, and pudding. He wished desperately for one of those sandwiches. Would it not be wonderful if he could sit in one of the shops and enjoy a nice warm dinner? Poor Tom felt quite sad that day. He went home that night—wet and cold—and went directly to bed. All night his dreams were about palaces and princes and huge dinners. He dreamed that he was the prince and everything belonged to him. When he woke up in the morning and saw the poverty and dirt around him, Tom felt even sadder. He lay on his straw mat and cried.

CHAPTER 2

Two Worlds Collide

ᘓ

Tom got up from his straw mat. He was hungry and in a daze. He left his home without a word and started walking down the street. Tom was lost in his thoughts. It was quite some time later that he realized how far he had wandered. He had never been so far from home before. He didn't stop, though. He continued on his way.

Tom walked through the gates of the city and into the countryside. He walked along the city wall. In the distance, he saw a great palace. It was Westminster, where King Henry lived. It was also where Prince Edward lived. Tom wondered if he would have the chance to see the real prince.

There were guards standing on either side of the palace gate. They stood perfectly still and straight. There were a few other people gathered nearby hoping to catch a glimpse of royalty. Tom watched as the gates opened and several beautiful carriages left the palace grounds. He was sure they were carrying elegant and splendid people.

Tom approached the gates slowly. He was very aware of the rags he was wearing and the dirt on his face. He knew that he stood out from the rest of the crowd, but his curiosity was too strong. One can only imagine how his heart skipped a beat when he noticed a small group inside the grounds. At the center of the group was a young boy wearing satins and silks, with a jeweled sword at his side. Tom knew at once that this was the prince. At long last, it was Prince Edward in the flesh!

Tom's eyes grew wide with excitement. His desire to see the prince up close became even stronger. He was no longer aware of the other people around him. The guards and other palace visitors disappeared. Without even realizing it, Tom pressed his face against the bars of the gate. He was so slender that he almost slipped through.

Suddenly he felt a firm hand grab his arm. "Step back, beggar!" the guard yelled. "Mind your manners."

The crowd laughed and pointed at Tom. "That's right!" they called. "Keep your distance, beggar!"

"Leave him alone!" The voice came from inside the palace grounds. "How dare you insult one of my father's subjects?" The young prince rushed toward the gates to help Tom. He was furious. "Open the gates and let him in! I will not stand by while anyone is treated so roughly."

The crowd stopped laughing and pointing.

They took off their hats and bowed before their prince. "Long live the Prince of Wales!" they called.

The guards opened the gates so Tom could enter. They watched as the Prince of Poverty in his rags ran past them to greet the Prince of Plenty in his expensive robes.

Edward looked at Tom. "You look tired and hungry," he said. "I'm sorry my guard was so rough with you. Please come with me."

Several guards stepped forward as Tom started to follow Edward. The prince waved them aside. No one else tried to stop Tom from going with the prince.

Edward led Tom inside the palace. He spoke to the servants in the hallway, telling them to bring lunch to his room. Tom was speechless. The palace was more beautiful than he had ever imagined.

The prince's room was amazing. There was a fireplace with a roaring fire, a rug on the floor, and large comfortable chairs. Sunshine poured in through the clean glass windows. Before Tom had a moment to look around the room, the servants arrived with lunch.

Tom had never seen anything like it before. He had read about feasts in books, but it was very different to see one with his own eyes. There was fruit and cold meat and loaves of bread. Tom stared at the table not knowing what he should do.

Edward noticed that Tom was uncomfortable. "Please have a seat. Help yourself to whatever you would like." The prince pulled out a chair so Tom could sit down.

"What is your name?" the prince asked as he sat at the table.

"Tom Canty."

"Do you live near here?"

"No," Tom said. It was difficult for him to talk. He was enjoying the food so much, but he didn't want to speak with his mouth full. "I live quite far from here in Offal Court."

"Offal Court?" The prince repeated. "I've never heard of such a place. Is it nice?"

"Well," Tom thought carefully before answering, "it's very different from your home."

"And do you have parents?" The prince was very curious about this strange boy. He had never met anyone like him before. His clothes were rags and he wore no shoes on such a chilly winter day.

"Yes. I have a mother, a father, and two older sisters. My grandmother lives with us, too."

The prince noticed that Tom looked sad as he spoke. "Do they treat you well?" the prince asked.

"My mother is very kind," Tom replied. "So are my sisters, Nan and Bet." Tom paused. He looked to the prince and decided it was best to be honest. "My father and grandmother are not so kind. When they are angry—which happens quite often—they yell at me. They send me to bed without supper, too."

"What!" The prince stood up. His eyes were afire. "Do you mean that they starve you?"

Tom hung his head. "Yes, Sir," he said very quietly.

"That is awful! I will not let this continue. I will speak to my father and have those awful people arrested."

"I think your father might have more important things to do," Tom said.

"Nonsense," Edward said. He waved his hand. "I will not let this unfairness pass." Edward looked at the boy in rags. "You know, my father has quite a bad temper. He has never yelled at me, but I've seen him get very angry with other people. It's quite awful to watch."

Tom smiled. It was nice that they had something in common.

"Does your family have many servants?" Edward asked.

"My goodness, no," Tom said. He almost laughed, but he knew that would be rude.

The prince was shocked. "But how do your sisters undress themselves at night? And who helps them get dressed in the morning?"

"They have to do that all on their own, I'm afraid. But, they only have one dress each, so there isn't too much trouble."

"You can't be telling me the truth?" Edward looked shocked again.

"Well, they each only have one body," Tom replied.

"I will take care of it. Your sisters shall soon have more dresses than they've ever dreamed of. I will see to it immediately." Edward noticed Tom's look of surprise. "Don't worry, there's no need to thank me." He waved his hand again.

"I must say, Tom," Edward added. "You speak very well. Have you been to school?"

"No," Tom said. "But one of my neighbors is a priest. He taught me to read and write. He even taught me some Latin. I don't know many words, I'm afraid, but I'm still learning."

"You should stick with it," Edward said. "It will become easier with practice."

Edward sat quietly for a moment. "Sometimes it feels like I've spent my entire life in school. Long hours with tutors every day or learning about state business. They are preparing me to be the king one day. There is very little time for anything else." He looked at Tom. "What do you do when you aren't in school?"

"Well," Tom said, "my father forces me to beg in the streets for money. He gets very angry if I don't bring home enough, so I worry about that a lot."

Tom smiled at the prince. "I do have wonderful friends, though. There is always something to do. We watch puppet shows in the square. There are plays. Sometimes a musician with a pet monkey will entertain people in the street. We have races and play fights. In the summer, we go swimming in the river." Tom smiled again. "I think that is my favorite thing. Splashing about in the water makes me very happy."

It was now the prince's turn to look sad. "How I wish I could have a day like that! One day to play in the water and have races. One day when I didn't have to worry about lessons or royal duties."

Edward looked at Tom in his rags. "If only I could wear your clothes and enjoy your life for one day, nothing would make me happier."

Tom stared in amazement. "Sir, if I could wear your robes and clothes but once, I would never ask for another thing."

"Then let us do it!" The prince stood up. "Let's change our clothes. Perhaps it will only be for a few moments, but that should be long enough!"

A few minutes later, Tom was standing in the royal chambers wearing the prince's clothes.

Edward stood in front of him wearing the dirty rags of a pauper. The two boys walked to a mirror to look at themselves. They stood side-by-side and stared into the glass. Both boys were both shocked and amazed by what they saw.

"Look at us," Edward said slowly. "I didn't notice before how similar we look. We are the same height and have the same color hair and eyes. Why, we could be twins!"

"I see it, too, Your Majesty," Tom said. "I don't think anyone could tell us apart." The two boys continued to stare at each other.

"Wait a moment," Edward said, "is that a bruise on your arm? Is that from the palace guard grabbing you?"

"Yes, I'm afraid so," Tom replied. "You shouldn't worry, though. The guard was only doing—"

"Nonsense!" The prince waved his hand. "I

will take care of this right away. Please wait for me here. I'll only be a moment, I promise."

Edward grabbed some important things that were on his desk and quickly locked them away. Then he ran out the door and onto the palace grounds. Unfortunately, Edward forgot that he was still wearing Tom's rags. He ran straight to the gates and shouted, "Unlock these gates! I must speak with you."

The guard who had been so rough with Tom earlier in the day opened the gates. Then, just as Edward was about to speak, the guard pushed the boy onto the road. "Get away, beggar!"

The crowd laughed and pointed again.

"Hold on!" Edward shouted. "How dare you treat me this way! I am the prince of England!"

Everyone laughed even harder. They all bowed before Edward. "Oh, excuse us, Your Majesty." Someone pushed Edward and he fell down.

"How dare you touch me!" Edward was angry and confused. Why were they all laughing at him? He had never been treated this way before.

"Come on, then" the guard said. "Make way for the prince of England."

The crowd parted, and the guard pushed Edward farther down the road. "Keep moving, beggar! Don't let me see you near the palace again."

Poor Edward continued to protest, but no one believed him. Instead, the people kept laughing and shoving him. After a short while, the crowd grew tired of their game. They no longer found it funny that this beggar claimed to be the prince. Some turned away and left for home. Others yelled at Edward and shoved him roughly.

Eventually Edward realized that there was little point in arguing. He was trapped outside of his home with no hope of getting in. He walked along the road—not knowing where he was going—in the hopes that he might find some help.

CHAPTER 3

Edward Finds His Way
to Offal Court

⌒

Edward didn't recognize any of his surroundings. He knew he was in London, but he had never seen this neighborhood before. He stopped a policeman to explain the situation, but the policeman called him a brat and brushed him aside. Poor Edward was completely on his own. He used to dream of a time when he could be all alone, but now that he had his wish, he was terrified.

Just then it started to rain. The poor homeless prince continued his journey through the streets. Suddenly a man grabbed him by the collar.

"Out this late, are you?" the man said. "And you haven't even brought home a penny for your mother or me."

Edward pulled free and turned to face the man. "Are you his father? Are you Mr. Canty?" The man looked strangely at Edward. "Thank heavens you've found me. Now we can straighten this all out."

"'His father?'" Mr. Canty said. "What are you going on about, boy? I'm *your* father."

"Please, let us not delay anymore. I'm hurt, tired, and cold. Take me to my father the king right away."

Mr. Canty started to chuckle. "Well, it's finally happened. You've gone mad. Our Tom is crazy." Mr. Canty laughed. He enjoyed the suffering of others. "Enough of this," he said. He grabbed the prince's collar again and dragged him down the street.

Another man stepped up to them. Edward couldn't see him clearly in the dark street. He only noticed that the man was wearing a long robe.

"Leave the boy alone," the man said. "You're hurting him."

"You can't tell me how to treat my son!" Mr. Canty said, growing angry. His pride was hurt. He didn't like to be challenged.

"He's just a boy," the man said.

"Mind your own business," Mr. Canty hissed. He shoved the man, who landed on the cobblestones with a thud.

Mr. Canty grabbed the prince and pulled him roughly down the street. Edward struggled and called for help all the way back to the Canty's home.

CHAPTER 4

Tom's Adventures with Edward Gone

～

Left alone in the prince's room, Tom Canty found plenty to amuse him. He spent a long time looking at himself in the mirror. He turned first left and then right. He walked away, imitating the prince's walk. He looked behind him while he walked so he could see himself in the mirror. Tom pretended the room was filled with dukes and earls. He spoke to each of them about very important matters. When the imaginary dukes bowed before him, he told them to rise and waved his hand. Tom did his best to copy the prince's wave.

Eventually Tom realized that the prince had been gone for a long time. He was losing interest in picking things up and looking at them. He was also starting to feel very uncomfortable. What if someone came in and caught him in the prince's clothes? What was the punishment for imitating a prince?

Tom tiptoed to the door and opened it quietly. He peered out into the hallway. Six servants sitting in chairs sprang to their feet. "What can we do for you, Sir?" one of them asked.

Tom quickly stepped back into the room and shut the door. *They're making fun of me,* he thought to himself. *They'll be rushing to get the guards right now.* He paced up and down the room.

Just then the door opened and one of the servants announced, "Lady Jane Grey." A young girl in a beautiful dress bounded into the room. She rushed toward Tom, but stopped in her tracks when she saw the look on his face.

"My Lord," Lady Jane asked, "are you feeling all right?"

It was difficult for Tom to speak. He struggled to get the words out. "Oh, please, you must help me. I am no lord. I am not a prince. My name is Tom Canty, and I am here by mistake. The prince and I switched clothes. It was only supposed to be for a few minutes, but I don't know where he went. He should have been back a long time ago."

By this time, Tom was on his knees before Lady Jane. He clasped his hands and begged her to believe him.

Lady Jane cried out. "My Lord—on your knees? Sir, this is not acceptable." She turned from Tom and ran out of the room.

Tom was in despair. He sank to the floor in tears. "There is no hope. I will go to jail for sure, now."

Meanwhile, the rest of the palace was starting to panic. The word was quickly spreading that the prince had gone mad. He believed he was someone else and did not know Lady Jane. How could he not recognize a girl he had known all his life? Her father was a close friend of the king and the children spent a great deal of time together. The king had been ill for some time and was resting in his room. When the whispers about the prince's madness reached him, he sent for his son.

Poor Tom was led from the prince's room. He walked down several long hallways surrounded by doctors, servants, and members of the court. He was terrified. He had no idea what to expect. Surely the king would recognize him as a fake right away.

Soon Tom was standing in a warm and beautiful room. A large, round man with a beard was lying on a couch near the fireplace. He was a stern-looking man. A great many people were frightened of him, but his voice was gentle when he spoke to the boy.

"How are you, my son?" King Henry asked. "You gave Lady Jane quite a fright."

"Y-You are the king?" Tom stuttered. "Then this must be my end." The boy shook his head.

"Ah, Edward," the king sighed. "My boy. I hoped the stories were not true, but I can see that you are deeply troubled. Come closer to me, my son." Henry gently took the boy's face in his hands. "Do you not recognize your own dear father?" The king looked at him closely. "It breaks my heart that you might not know me."

"I assume that you are my king," Tom answered.

The king could feel the boy tremble. "Please do not be afraid. There is no one here who will hurt you."

"P-please, Sir, you must believe me. I speak the truth. I am not Prince Edward. My name is Tom Canty, and I am a beggar from Offal Court. It's a mistake that I am here. I don't know where Prince

Edward is right now." Tom began to cry. "I don't want to go to jail! Please, I just want to go home to my family and friends!

"Jail?" King Henry asked. "My poor sweet boy. Of course you won't go to jail. Why would you think such a thing? Why would I want to punish you? You are always free to go and do what you want."

"Then I am free to go?" Tom asked. He was very excited.

"You may leave whenever you'd like. Although I wish you could stay a few minutes more," King Henry said. He looked closely at Tom. "Where would you go?"

"I would go back to my home, of course. My friends and family in Offal Court must be looking for me by now." Tom was excited that this ordeal would soon be over.

The king dropped his head. "My son is mad," he said. "Heaven bless us, but the prince of England is mad. He does not know who he is."

The king looked at the doctors and court officials in the room. They all looked worried. "I am telling you all right now that sane or mad, my son will one day be the king of England."

The king's chief advisor stepped forward. His name was Lord Hertford. He helped the king with his work and was almost always at Henry's side. "The king's will is law," he said and bowed before the king and Tom.

The king sighed again. "I must rest now." He laid his head against his pillow. "Edward, my boy, go with your Uncle Hertford now. Come and see me later when I am refreshed."

Lord Hertford led Tom away. He passed down the halls again and returned to the prince's room. For so long Tom had dreamed of life in the palace—of living the life of a prince—but his dream was quickly turning into a nightmare.

CHAPTER 5

Tom Learns the
Rules of the Palace

～

Later that afternoon, Lord Hertford brought a
group of men to the prince's room. He pointed
to a chair and indicated that Tom should sit. The
boy did as he was told, but he felt strange. He
knew that it was not polite to sit when his superi-
ors were standing. He asked that they sit as well.
The men all bowed their heads but remained
standing.

Tom was about to insist when Lord Hertford
whispered in his ear, "Your Majesty, do not press

the matter. It is not proper for them to sit in your presence.

"I'm sorry, Your Majesty, but we need to speak for a moment," Lord Hertford continued. He stood in front of Tom. "I'm sure you know how important it is for the people of England to have faith in their king."

Tom nodded slowly.

"And I'm sure you understand that your father's illness has many people worried." Lord Hertford watched as Tom nodded his head again. "Your father has given orders that you should not cause any more problems. He has asked that you no longer mention this boy Tom Canty or Offal Court."

Tom nodded. He knew there was nothing he could say. He felt trapped in the prince's clothes.

As he watched, Lord Hertford and the men carried out business. Tom listened and nodded in agreement when Hertford indicated that he should. Then all the men except Lord Hertford left, and Princess Elizabeth and Lady Jane walked in. They were both in good spirits.

Lord Hertford leaned in to whisper in Tom's ear. "I ask that you keep your father's wishes in mind, Prince Edward. We wouldn't want to alarm anyone further."

Tom nodded again and quietly answered, "Yes."

Then he turned his attention to Elizabeth and Jane. The two girls were lively and interesting. Their presence helped take Tom's mind off his problems. But, it was not entirely easy for him. The girls spoke of things and people that he didn't know. Occasionally they spoke to him in languages that he didn't understand. Elizabeth noticed that he was having a hard time. She did her best to help him when he was confused. She even held his hand when he looked upset. Tom knew that no matter what happened to him while he was stuck in the palace, he would always be glad to have met Elizabeth and Jane.

After the girls left, Tom realized that he was tired. It had been a long day. He asked Lord Hertford and the others in the room if he could be alone for a while.

"Of course," Lord Hertford said. "It is for you to command and for us to obey."

Everyone left the room except the servants. Tom waited for them to exit as well. "Thank you for your help," he said, "but I think I'll take a nap now."

"Of course, Sir," one of them said. He took hold of Tom's cape and began to undo the buttons.

Tom realized that they were there to help him undress. He remembered Prince Edward's surprise that his sisters didn't have help dressing and undressing. Tom decided not to argue. Instead, he accepted their help with a big sigh.

After his nap, Tom suffered the same ordeal again—although this time in reverse. Rather than being undressed for his nap, he was redressed in expensive and heavy clothes for dinner. Then one of the servants led him into a large room with one long table. He sat at one end of the table in a large, comfortable chair.

Although Tom was dining alone, he was not alone in the room. He was surrounded by servants and servers. Tom thought it odd that although he finally had enough to eat, it was hard to enjoy the meal.

He looked at his napkin. It was made of a frail and delicate fabric. Colorful thread lined the edges. It was quite beautiful. "Please take this away," he said to the butler. "I wouldn't want to dirty it."

The butler took the napkin from Tom without a comment.

The servants watched Tom while he ate. It was

hard to see their prince in such a state. He used the wrong fork when eating his salad, he slurped from his cup, and he poked at his vegetables. Tom had never seen turnips before or the green leaf called lettuce. The servants watched in horror as Tom put down his fork and ate the rest of his meal with his hands.

Midway through his meal, Tom discovered a new problem. His nose was itchy and he didn't know what to do. Should he scratch it himself? If he wasn't allowed to dress himself, was he allowed to scratch his own nose?

"Pardon me," Tom said, "can someone please tell me if I am allowed to scratch my nose?" All of the servants stared at him in disbelief. No one knew what to do, so they remained quiet. Eventually Tom gave up and did his own scratching.

At the end of dinner, Tom stood up. He filled his pockets with nuts—in case he was hungry later—and headed back to his room. "Thank you for the meal," Tom said. "Have a good night." He waved to everyone and left the room.

The servants watched Tom leave. They hoped their prince's illness would not last long.

CHAPTER 6

The Matter of the Royal Seal

❦

King Henry woke from his nap in a state of panic. He knew that he was dying and wanted to make sure that everything would run smoothly when he was gone. The king of England had so many responsibilities. What if Edward had trouble? Was his son feeling too much stress? Was that why he was speaking so strangely?

King Henry called Lord Hertford to his room. He was one of the king's most trusted friends. He knew almost all of the king's business. In fact, he was among the few people who knew how long the king had been sick. He also knew that Prince Edward had been taking over some of the king's work.

"We need to finish our work," King Henry said. "We'll need the royal seal to complete these new laws." Henry was finding it difficult to breathe. He spoke very slowly to save his strength. "I loaned the seal to Prince Edward a few days ago. Please get it from him."

"Of course, Your Majesty," Hertford said. He went straight to Prince Edward's room.

When he got there, Hertford found Tom working on his Latin homework. He appeared to be studying very hard. Hertford wondered if the prince's sick mind made it more difficult to learn.

"Sir, your father sent me," Hertford said and bowed before Tom. "He asked that I bring the royal seal to him."

Tom looked up from his textbook. He was very confused. What on Earth was a royal seal? "I beg your pardon, Lord Hertford," Tom said, "but I don't understand."

"The royal seal," Hertford tried again. "Your father loaned it to you last week. We need it to finish some important business."

Tom looked around the room. Would he even recognize the seal if he saw it? "Can you describe it to me?" he asked quietly. Poor Tom knew he was disappointing Hertford, but he was doing the best he could.

"It has a handle and a gold disk at the bottom."

Tom shook his head. "No, I'm sorry. I haven't seen that." He thought for a moment. "Perhaps the true prince already returned it." Tom noticed the look on Hertford's face. "I mean, perhaps I returned it last week."

Hertford spent the next few minutes trying to convince Tom that the royal seal—whatever it may be—was somewhere in the room. Tom just smiled and shrugged his shoulders.

Well, Hertford thought as he walked back to the king's room, *the prince may be mad but at least he's still polite.*

When Hertford told King Henry that the royal seal was lost, the king sighed heavily. "I hope my son recovers quickly. It simply won't do to have a mad prince, let alone a mad king."

CHAPTER 7

Edward's First Night Away from the Palace

Meanwhile, life outside of the palace continued for Prince Edward. While Tom was learning how to act as a prince, Edward was learning how hard it was to be poor. He was not used to having people ignore him. They usually jumped at his every command. Yet he could not make Mr. Canty listen to him.

John Canty dragged the pleading prince into the family's room. Edward fought and yelled, but Canty held on tight.

"I've had enough of you and your back talk," Mr. Canty scowled. "I want you out on the streets and begging for money by dawn tomorrow! And stay out there. There's no time for play or seeing your friends."

"Leave the boy alone!" Mrs. Canty shouted.

Canty looked at his wife in amazement. "How dare you speak to me that way. I will do as I like in my own home." He let go of the boy, though, and told him to get to bed.

Edward looked about the room. It was lit by a single candle and was quite dark. An old woman sat in the corner. Two girls sitting nearby looked at him with pity. They tried to smile, but they looked worried.

"I'll have you all know," he said to Mr. Canty, "that this treatment will not go unnoticed. I am Edward, Prince of Wales. You will pay for your actions when I am returned to the palace."

Everyone in the room looked at Edward. The old woman in the corner started to laugh. "The boy's finally gone over the edge!" She rocked in her chair, cackling to herself.

Mrs. Canty looked at the boy with sympathy. "Oh, my dear son," she said. "Do you feel ill?" She reached for his forehead to check for a fever. She started to cry as she stroked his cheek. "Oh my poor sweet Tom."

"I am sorry," Edward said softly. "My name is not Tom. It is Edward. Prince Edward." He realized immediately that she was a very kind woman. He did not want to frighten her more. "Your son is fine. Please don't worry. He is at the palace right now. We exchanged clothes—"

"Well aren't we the lucky ones," Mr. Canty interrupted. "Not everyone on Offal Court gets a royal visit." He looked at the old woman and winked. She continued to laugh.

"Come on. Nan! Bet! Don't sit in front of the

prince. Don't you know that's rude?" Mr. Canty stood with his hands on his hips. "We wouldn't want the prince to think badly of us." When the girls did not move, Mr. Canty became angry. "You heard me!" he shouted. "You should kneel before your prince."

"Father," Nan said, "Tom is very tired. We should let him get some sleep."

"I'm sure he will be better in the morning," Bet added.

"And another day's wages down the drain!" the old woman said.

Edward stood up. "Enough of this! I am the king's son."

Mr. Canty looked at Edward. His face was red with rage.

Mrs. Canty took the boy in her arms. "Please," she said softly, "let him sleep through the night. It will all be better in the morning."

Mr. Canty looked at his wife. "Fine," he said.

"We'll leave it be for now. But only because I'm tired from my day."

Mrs. Canty nodded her head. She stroked Edward's hair. "Come, my boy. Lie down and try to sleep." Mrs. Canty straightened the blankets on the straw mat and tucked Edward in. She tried to make him as comfortable as possible. She took a piece of bread that she had saved for him out of her pocket.

"Thank you, Mrs. Canty," Edward whispered. "I will always remember your kindness."

When everyone else was safely sleeping, Mrs. Canty rose and stood beside Edward. She watched him sleep for a few minutes. It seemed impossible that this was not her boy. Yet there was something that did not feel quite right. Perhaps it was his tone of voice or how he held his head. Maybe it was the way he waved his arm when he did not like something. It was as if he were pushing unwanted people or thoughts aside.

She knew Tom's gestures and habits as well as she knew her own. Whenever he was woken from a deep sleep, he held his hand in front of his face with his palm out. He had done it a thousand times, and it was always the same.

Mrs. Canty knelt beside the boy. Using a feather from her mattress, she tickled his nose. The boy's eyes opened wide and he sat up slightly, but he did not put his hand in front of his face. Instead, he closed his eyes and fell back into a deep sleep. Just to be certain, Mrs. Canty tickled his nose with the feather again. The boy did not open his eyes this time. He merely rolled over and pulled the blanket closer.

Mrs. Canty didn't know if she should laugh or cry. She was happy to realize this boy was not her son. It meant that Tom was not mad, but she was worried. Was her boy safe? Was he truly in the palace? Surely the king would notice that something was different. Perhaps she was mad. How could this not be her son? None of it made any sense to her.

Mrs. Canty returned to her bed. *All of this must be a dream,* she thought. *All will be normal in the morning.*

The next morning, however, was anything but normal. Everyone in the tiny room was awakened by shouting outside. Suddenly there were several sharp raps on the door.

"Who's there?" Mr. Canty shouted from his bed. "What do you want?"

"You'd better get a move on, Canty," a man said. "You're in a lot of trouble. That man you knocked down last night was the old priest, Father Andrew. You hit him too hard. They've taken him to the hospital. The police are heading this way."

Mr. Canty jumped up. There was no time to waste! "Come on, everyone up! We're leaving this minute."

Edward sat up, startled and confused. What on Earth was all that noise? It took him a few minutes to remember where he was—that he was no longer in the palace. His heart sank into his stomach again.

Before he knew it, Edward was racing down the staircase with the Cantys. The streets were crowded and full of excitement. There was a street festival. There were games, musicians, and bonfires along the riverbank. And the royal boat was out on the water! It was just as Tom had described it to the prince. Unfortunately, Edward had no time to enjoy it.

Mr. Canty grabbed Edward's hand to pull him through the crowd. Mrs. Canty, Nan, Bet, and the old woman followed behind. They were all bumped and pushed by the excited crowd.

Mr. Canty lost his balance and almost fell to the ground. He needed both hands to balance himself. As soon as he let go of Edward's hand, the prince slipped past the crowd and disappeared. In only a few moments, he was free of his pretend father and was running along the riverside.

CHAPTER 8

Long Live the King of England!

~

As the royal boat made its way down the river Thames, Tom sat on a throne. The throne was much higher than anything else on the boat. From his seat, Tom had a wonderful view of the street festival. He had never seen the fair from the water before. He was surprised at how beautiful it looked.

Tom looked over at Elizabeth and Jane. They were talking to each other. They didn't notice the lights on shore or the people singing. Tom realized that they must have seen this view of the fair many times before. It wasn't so special to them.

The boat docked and Tom, Elizabeth, and Jane were helped ashore. As they walked over to a large hall, the crowd parted to make way for the royal trio. Trumpets played as they walked through the door. Everyone bowed. A group of guards led Tom and the girls to seats on a stage. Once the three children were seated, everyone else took their seats.

The hall was quiet for only a few minutes. Then a celebration began. Tom watched from his chair on the stage. It was an incredible sight. People started to dance. Colors twirled around each other. For a while Tom forgot all about his troubles. He forgot that he was trapped as the prince, that no one believed him, and that he would surely go to jail if anyone found out the truth. He was happily lost in the sights and sounds of the party.

How strange that while Tom was enjoying the delights of the party, the real prince of England was outside the hall trying desperately to get in. Edward did his best to convince the guards that he was the true prince, but they refused to listen. The crowd around him laughed, of course. Edward wondered if he would ever get used to this type of laughter. He had heard it too many times in the past two days. He was quite certain that he did not like it.

"You must believe me," Edward said. "I am the true Prince of Wales! It is a fraud who sits inside."

"Get away, boy" a woman said. She was trying to look inside the hall.

"Don't let them bother you," a man said. "Whether you are the real prince or not, they have no right to treat you that way."

Edward looked up to see a tall, thin man beside him. Although his clothes had seen better days, he was well dressed. His coat was covered with patches and mismatched buttons. He had a kind face, though. He smiled at Edward.

"My name is Miles Hendon," the man said. He held a hand toward Edward.

The boy did not take his hand. He nodded instead. "My name is Edward," he said.

"Yes, of course," Miles replied. "It is a pleasure to meet you, Prince Edward." Miles bowed before Edward. "Let me talk to this guard for you."

When the crowd heard Miles defending the boy, they started to laugh. "Oh look! It's another prince in disguise!"

"Maybe we should help them," someone else said.

"Yes," the first man said. "I think they do need some help. They need some help into the pond."

Everyone laughed. Suddenly Edward felt a hand on his arm. Someone was pulling him farther into the crowd. He let out a cry and Miles pulled out his sword.

The man who was holding onto Edward's arm let go. He backed away from Miles and the boy.

"Leave him alone," Miles said. "He's none of your concern."

Others in the crowd did not seem as willing to back down. They moved toward Miles. They did not seem afraid of his sword.

Suddenly a trumpet sounded. "Make way for the king's messenger," the trumpeter called as a man appeared near the gates of the hall. Everyone turned to watch as the man walked inside. Miles took this opportunity to grab Edward and carry him off to safety. Unfortunately, this meant that they missed the messenger's news—news that would have been of great interest to the boy.

Inside the hall, all the partygoers stopped to listen as the king's messenger approached. Poor Tom. He had been perfectly happy just to sit and watch the dancers. This had been a strange day, but he was enjoying himself. When he finally woke up from his daydream, he realized that everyone in the room was watching him. They were all waiting for him to say that the messenger could speak.

The trumpet sounded once more, and the messenger cleared his throat. "The king is dead!" he said. The room was silent. Everyone—most importantly Tom—stared in silence. "The king is dead!" the messenger said again.

Everyone in the room bowed their heads and said a silent prayer. Then they turned to Tom. They lifted glasses or raised their hands. "Long live the king!" they all cheered.

Poor Tom had no idea what to do. He looked about the room for a friendly face—someone to tell him what to do—but everyone was looking to him to make the next move. They were all cheering for the future king.

Tom leaned over to Hertford and whispered in his ear. "Is it true that I will soon be crowned king?" Tom asked.

"Yes, Your Majesty," Hertford said. "In a few short weeks you will be named king of all of England. Until then, you and I will go over all the details together. I will help you ease into your new position. By the time you are crowned, you will know everything there is to know about being king."

Tom sat in his chair feeling miserable. The future king of England! Whatever was he to do?

CHAPTER 9

Edward and Miles Learn More

Edward should have been the one speaking with Lord Hertford. He should have been the one the crowd cheered. Instead, he was running through the streets of London, trying to find safety.

Miles led Edward through the back streets and alleys. He held onto the prince's arm tightly. More and more people were flooding into the streets. Miles didn't understand all the excitement. He was surprised that the street fair was so big. By the time they reached the London Bridge, the streets were filled with people.

Edward learned the news of his father's death from the cheers and shouts of the crowd. They called, "The king is dead! Long live the king! Long live King Edward!"

Tears came to the boy's eyes. This man who was often so mean to others had always been gentle with him. It upset him to know that his father was dead and he had not said good-bye.

"I am now king," Edward said quietly. He looked at the cheering crowd around him. "I am now King Edward. Isn't it strange that no one can see me?"

Miles and Edward walked over the bridge. There were so many people on it that their movement was very slow. The bridge was always a busy place. It was lined with stores, inns, butcher shops, and bakeries. In fact, it was like a small city all on its own. Miles was staying at one of these inns. He and Edward were just about to walk through the front door when John Canty grabbed Edward from behind.

Mr. Canty had been looking for his son all day. He had crossed the bridge many times and asked everyone he knew if they had seen the boy. At last he had spotted him walking with Miles.

"So you thought you could escape," Mr. Canty hissed. He was furious. "I'll teach you a lesson—a lesson you will not soon forget." He pulled Edward by the arm, trying to take him down the street.

Miles stepped between them. "What do you have to do with this boy?" he asked. "Why are you threatening him?"

"What business is it of yours?" Mr. Canty's eyes narrowed. "He is my son, and I will do as I please."

"That's a lie!" Edward said. "He is not my

father. My father is the king. Or rather, my father was the king." Edward looked sad for a moment, but he quickly calmed himself. "This is a cruel and heartless man."

"Don't make me angry, boy," Mr. Canty said. "Don't try my patience."

"I will not go with him!" Edward said.

"Well, that settles it," Miles said. "The boy stays with me." He crossed his arms and held his ground.

"We'll see about that," Mr. Canty said as he reached for Edward.

"Mark my words," Miles said slowly. "This boy is now under my protection. No one will harm him. No one will force him do anything he doesn't want to do. For your own safety, I suggest you leave him alone." Miles rested his hand on his sword and stared at Mr. Canty.

Mr. Canty mumbled under his breath and walked away.

"It should be all right now," Miles said. He put his hand on the boy's shoulder. "We'll get a good night's sleep, at least."

Edward followed Miles up three flights of stairs to his room. By this time, it was very late at night. Edward was hungry and tired.

"Good sir, please let me know when the servants have brought in the evening meal," he said. Then he lay down on the bed. "I am very hungry, I'm afraid. I don't think I've eaten anything for a day or two."

Before Miles could even reply, Edward was fast asleep.

Miles smiled. *This boy may only be imagining he is the Prince of Wales, but he certainly knows how to behave like royalty. He just took my bed without even asking.* Miles looked about the room for an extra blanket, but there was none. He took off his jacket and used it to cover Edward.

Poor boy, Miles thought. *He is sick and confused, and*

doesn't have a friend in the world. Miles watched the boy as he slept. He looked so helpless. Miles thought about his own family. He had not seen them in years. He wondered if his father was still alive. His brothers, Arthur and Hugh, would have changed so much in the seven years since he had last spoken to them. Perhaps he should bring the boy back to his home. His father would welcome the sick boy with open arms. His brother Arthur would also be kind. Hugh might be more of a problem. Hugh had not been a nice person, but Miles hoped he had changed over the years.

Miles looked at Edward and said, "Well, I'll be his friend. After all, I am already his defender. Now I will act as his brother, too. Anyone who tries to harm him will have to deal with me first."

Just then a servant arrived with dinner. He left it on the table and then slammed the door on his way out. The young prince was startled awake. He sat up quickly, confused by his surroundings.

He looked sad. "Alas, I thought perhaps it was all a dream. This is the second morning in a row that I've been disappointed."

"It's not actually morning, Sire," Miles said. If the boy believed he was the Prince of Wales, then he would treat him as such. "It's still the middle of the night."

Edward noticed that Miles had used his coat to cover him. "You are too kind to me," he said to Miles. He held the coat out to the man. "Please take it back. I will need it no longer."

Miles took the coat from Edward. This was the first kind thing the boy had said. Miles wondered how long this politeness would last.

Edward stood up. He walked to the washstand in the corner and waited.

"We have some good food to enjoy," Miles said. "Perhaps not what you are used to at the palace, but it's warm and hearty. We can have a bite and then take a nap. We'll be rested and ready in the morning. We'll have to get an early start if we're to get you back to the palace."

Edward looked at Miles with surprise and a bit of impatience.

"Is something wrong?" Miles asked.

"I would like to wash up," Edward said.

"Oh, of course," Miles said. "Please feel free. You don't need to ask permission."

The boy stood still. He cleared his throat and tapped his foot.

"I'm sorry, I don't understand," Miles said. "Is there anything else?"

"Please pour the water into the bowl," Edward said sternly. His voice was full of authority. "And, use fewer words, please."

Miles caught himself before bursting into laughter. He nodded politely and then did as Edward had asked.

He waited patiently as Edward washed himself. *This boy has some nerve*, he thought to himself. *He truly does believe he is Prince Edward. He would surely be hurt if I left him on his own. After all, I've already had to defend him twice within a single night.*

Miles was startled from his thoughts by the command, "Come—towel!"

Although it was well within Edward's reach, Miles handed him the towel that sat beside the washstand. Miles then washed himself while Edward sat down at the table to eat.

When Miles was finished washing up, he moved to the table. He pulled out a chair and prepared to sit.

"Hold on!" Edward said. "Do you dare to sit in the presence of the future king?"

Miles decided that there was only one way to handle this situation. He would humor the boy. There seemed no point in fighting him. The boy's mind was clearly disturbed. *If I cause any more trouble*, Miles laughed to himself, *he'll send me to the Tower of London*. So Miles did as the future king asked. He waited on him hand and foot during the meal.

When Edward finished eating, he leaned back in his chair. It was good to eat a solid meal at last. He felt much more relaxed. "Miles," he said. "That is your name, isn't it?"

"Yes, Sir. Miles Hendon."

"Have a seat, Miles." Edward waved his hand to indicate where Miles should sit. "Tell me about yourself while I digest my dinner."

Miles sat down. Edward waved his hand again—this time over the food to indicate that Miles should have something to eat. Miles held back another smile.

"I come from Kent. My father is Sir Richard Hendon of Hendon Hall."

"Ah, then you are nobly born," Edward said.

Miles nodded. "My family is quite wealthy. My father is a kind, generous man. He is well-loved by all the people who live in his district. My mother died when I was very young. I have two brothers. Arthur, who is older than I, takes after my father. He, too, is kind and generous. My younger brother, Hugh, is not as kind. At least he wasn't when last I saw him. I can only hope that he has changed for the better over the years. He was only nineteen then, so I am very hopeful.

"The Lady Edith also lived with us. She was but sixteen when last I saw her. Edith is beautiful, sweet, and intelligent. Her father was an earl who died when she was very young. My father became her guardian. Edith is the heiress to a great fortune. I loved Edith dearly, and she loved me. Unfortunately, she was engaged to my brother Arthur. It was an arranged marriage between the two families. Neither Arthur nor Edith had a choice in the matter. It was only out of loyalty to the families that they didn't protest.

"Arthur was in love with another woman. He was always optimistic that we would make it all work out. We just needed to be patient. Hugh claimed to love Edith too, but in truth he only loved her fortune. My brother Hugh was very persuasive, especially with our father. Sir Richard believed every word Hugh said. Although no one else trusted Hugh, our father thought he could do no wrong.

"To make a long story short, Hugh told our father lies about me. He said I was up to no good and that I was causing trouble and bringing shame to our family. Our brother Arthur was not healthy. He was born sickly, and we were always worried that he wouldn't have a long life. I believe Hugh thought it best to have me out of the way. I was next in line to inherit everything, including Edith's hand in marriage. He knew that he would have no claim on our father's or Edith's fortune if I was still around. Hugh convinced our father that I meant to kidnap Lady Edith and steal her fortune. My father reacted as any honorable man would when faced with such 'truths.' He banished me from our home. I was sent off for military service—three years with the army.

"It was a difficult three years, and I faced many battles. I also learned a great deal. My punishment was unfair, but I made the most of it. Then I was taken prisoner. I have spent the past seven years in a foreign prison camp. I managed to escape at long last and make my way back to England. I have had no word from my family in all this time. I don't know if my father and Arthur are still alive or if my brother Hugh has at long last changed.

"I have only been back in England for a few

THE PRINCE AND THE PAUPER

days. I was on my way to my father's house when
I found you," Miles said.

"You have been shamefully abused!" Edward
said. "When I return to my throne, I will right this
terrible wrong. You have my word!"

"Thank you, Sire," Miles said. "That is very
kind of you."

"Think nothing of it," Edward said with a
wave of his hand. "Now let me tell you how I—
the king of England—am dressed in rags and
walking the streets of London."

While Edward spoke, Miles felt great pity for
the boy. *His mind is completely crazed*, he thought. *He
has lost touch with reality. He needs me to care for him more
than I suspected.*

When Edward finished his tale, Miles shook
his head in amazement. "That is a terrible story,
Sire," he said.

"You have saved me tonight," Edward said. "I

will not forget it. Tell me your greatest wish. When I am crowned king, you shall have your heart's desire."

Miles thought carefully for a few moments. His first instinct was to simply say that it was honor enough to be of service. It occurred to Miles, though, that since he was not likely to enjoy his reward, he might as well ask for the Moon.

He dropped to his knees before Edward. "I ask but one thing, Your Majesty, that I—and all my heirs—always have the pleasure of sitting in the royal court."

"Your wish shall be granted," Edward said. "And you will forever be known as Sir Miles Hendon."

Suddenly Edward realized that he was very tired. "And now remove these rags," he said. He pointed to his clothes. "It is time for sleep. It has been a very long day."

Edward slipped into bed, preparing to sleep. "Sleep in front of the door, Miles," he said. "In case we have intruders."

Miles barely had a chance to answer before Edward was sound asleep again. *He really should have been born a king*, he thought. *He plays the part so well.*

Miles stretched out in front of the door. *Well, I've certainly slept in worse places over the past seven years.*

When Miles awoke, it was already noon. This was much later than he had intended to sleep. Now they would have to hurry. He stood up and prepared to go outside. Edward stirred and asked what he was doing. "Just taking care of a bit of business, Sire," Miles replied. "I'll be back shortly. Please don't trouble yourself." Edward was sound asleep again before Miles was out the door.

He returned thirty minutes later with a second-hand suit for Edward and some breakfast. He sat down at the table to make a few repairs to the suit. One of the hems was falling down and a button needed refastening. While he worked, Miles looked over at the bed. He noticed for the first time—to his great surprise and horror—that Edward was gone!

Miles raced downstairs. He ran straight up to the servant who brought their dinner in the night before and shouted, "Where is the boy?"

The servant was frightened by Miles's anger. He found it difficult to speak. "Another boy came to the door after you left, sir," the man stuttered. "He said that you wanted the young boy from your room to meet you near the bridge. So I went to your room and woke him up. He was upset about being woken up so early, but he dressed and came downstairs."

"Did Edward leave with this other boy?" Miles asked.

"Yes," the servant said. "They walked off together toward the bridge."

"Is that all you remember? Is there anything else that will help me find him?" Miles hoped this youth meant Edward no harm.

"There was one strange bit," the servant said quietly. "I watched them as they walked off. About half a block away, a rather dirty man stepped out from a doorway and joined them. He grabbed your young friend's arm and pulled him toward the bridge. I assumed you were quite anxious to see him."

"You fool!" Miles said. "How will I ever find him now?"

Miles rushed out the door of the inn. He ran up the street where the servant had last seen

Edward. *Poor lad*, Miles thought. *He might be in grave danger. It must have been that man who claims to be his father. How can I forgive myself? I should have kept a better eye on him. The poor boy is ill. Who knows what harm may come him. He went out because he thought I asked for him. He trusted me and now he may be lost!*

Miles ran as fast as he could. He had to find Edward before anything bad happened.

CHAPTER 10

Edward Is Trapped Again

ᥫᶆ

Miles searched the streets for Edward. He raced along the bridge. He ran from one end to the other, stopping people along the way to ask if they had seen Mr. Canty or the boy. He was able to follow their trail for a few blocks, but then he lost them. No one had seen them. No one knew where they were.

Miles continued his search throughout the day and into the night. He was tired, hungry, and had run out of leads. Finally he decided it was best to eat some supper and get a good night's sleep. He would start searching again in the morning.

Miles lay in bed thinking. He knew that Edward would try to escape from the man who claimed to be his father. *What would his next move be? Would he return to London? No. He was only risking recapture if he returned to this neighborhood. Was there anyone who the boy could depend upon? No.* Miles knew he was Edward's only protector. There was little Edward could do but search for his only friend. Since returning to London was out of the question, Edward's only option would be to head to Hendon Hall. Miles had told Edward that he was on his way to his family home. He would leave for Hendon Hall in the morning. He was certain he would find Edward along the way—or the young "future king" would find Miles at home.

Unfortunately, Edward was still in the clutches of Mr. Canty. But Mr. Canty was not alone this time. He had a young friend with him named Hugo. This new boy was also a thief. Edward was shocked and furious when he saw the horrible man. It was humiliating and insulting to be dragged through the streets. Mr. Canty was not looking very healthy. His arm was in a sling and he had a black eye. He was also limping slightly. With his one good arm, he held on to Edward and continued to pull.

Finally Edward stopped. He refused to go any farther. It was Miles who should come to him, not the other way around. "This is as far as I will go tonight." Edward said. "I have had enough."

"But your friend needs you," Mr. Canty said. "Your friend in the fancy coat." His voice was very sarcastic. "He's been wounded and is asking for you."

"Wounded?" Edward said. "Why didn't you say so sooner? Who would do such a thing?"

The trio continued walking. They went outside the walls of the city and into the woods. Finally they came to an old barn near a farmhouse. Mr. Canty, Hugo, and Edward all went inside. Edward looked all around him. "Where is he?" Edward said.

His answer was a mean laugh from Mr. Canty. "Well, you must be my son. You were fool enough to follow me into the woods. You should have known better than that."

"You are not my father," Edward said. "I have no idea what you are capable of. I ask you to be a good man and return me to the inn."

"I'm afraid not, my boy," Mr. Canty said. "The city isn't a safe place for me. I'm a wanted man, don't you know." He lifted his arm out of the sling and waved at Edward. "I'm in disguise. You never know where your enemies might be hiding."

Edward tried to back away, but Mr. Canty grabbed him again. "Tell me, boy. Where is your mother? Where are your sisters?"

Edward looked him straight in the eye. "Enough of these riddles. My mother is dead. My sisters are in the palace."

Hugo moved toward Edward. He looked as though he might shove the smaller boy, but Mr. Canty stopped him. "Leave him be, Hugo. There's no use wasting time on that boy."

While Mr. Canty and Hugo spoke in low voices, Edward walked to a dark corner of the barn. He fixed himself a bed in the straw and lay down. He ignored the sound of murmured voices. He thought about his father. If he did not make it back to the palace in time, he would miss his father's funeral. Edward remembered all the tender moments he had shared with the king. Even though he was sometimes distant, Henry had been a good father. Edward could not blame him for the distance. It was hard being the king of England. It took up a lot of one's time.

After a while, Edward's eyes began to droop. He was having trouble staying awake. He was just about to fall asleep when he heard louder noises coming from the other end of the barn. Mr. Canty and Hugo sat near a fire. Several other men and women were there as well. They were all laughing and talking loudly. Edward did not feel safe. They didn't look like very nice people.

Edward soon realized that Mr. Canty was old friends with this group. He listened to their stories of robberies and schemes. They talked about friends who had died, gone to jail, or worse. He also learned that some of this group did not choose to become thieves. They simply had nowhere else to turn when they lost their farms. They blamed the king, saying that Henry took their land but did not provide jobs for them. They had then tried begging in the street, but they were arrested. It was illegal to beg during the reign of King Henry. They had families to feed, so they turned to robbery. Edward wondered if these stories were true. Could his father have done such a terrible thing?

The "Boss"—or so everyone called him— stood up and lifted the back of his shirt. "See these scars?" he asked. "The prison guards gave these to me when I dared to complain. I said begging wasn't a crime, so they whipped me. Now if I go to jail, it will because I am a thief. If the punishment is the same, why not steal?"

"The laws will soon change!" Edward shouted across the barn. He walked toward the group. They all stared at him in amazement. No one except Hugo and his father knew he was there. "The laws will change as of this day!"

"Who is this?" the "Boss" asked Mr. Canty.

Mr. Canty shook his head. He was embarrassed. "He is my son. Pay no attention to him. Something has gone wrong with his mind. He thinks he is the king."

"I *am* the king," Edward said. He rushed toward Mr. Canty. "Soon you will not doubt me. Not only have you mistreated your family, you are also a thief. You will not go unpunished."

"Will you betray me, boy?" Mr. Canty hissed.

"I will bring you to justice," Edward said coldly. He was not frightened of this man.

"Now, now," the "Boss" said, "you may call yourself a king if you like, or you may call yourself a pauper. No one here will think one way or the other. But, we don't look kindly on people who snitch. We don't like tattletales."

Edward did not reply. He realized that this man did frighten him. He knew the "Boss" was dangerous.

"Now come, my brothers and sisters," the

"Boss" said to the rest of the group. "Give three cheers for the future king of England. It's not every day we have royalty with us."

"Long live Edward, the future king!" they all shouted. Everyone shouted, except Mr. Canty, that is. He sat with an angry look on his face.

"I thank you," Edward said.

This response made everyone in the barn roar with laughter. Even Mr. Canty smiled slightly.

"He deserves a better name than plain old Edward," a woman said. "Anyone can be an Edward."

"How about Foo Foo?" someone else suggested.

"That's perfect," the woman said. "Foo Foo the first!" Everyone cheered once more.

"He needs a crown," she called. She picked up a bowl and put it upside down on his head. Someone else draped a blanket over Edward's shoulders as a pretend robe.

"And a throne!" the woman said. They picked him up and set him on a barrel.

Everyone in the barn cheered and danced around Edward. They knelt before him and kissed his feet. Edward tried to push them aside. He yelled at them to stop, but it was useless. They couldn't hear him above their laughter. No one cared what he had to say.

CHAPTER 11

Edward Learns About the Life of a Thief

᠃

The thieves left the barn at dawn. Edward stood at the side of the road while some of the group broke into a farmhouse. No one was home, so they took what they wanted. They walked farther down the road, until they found another empty house, where they did the same thing.

Early that afternoon they came to a town. The "Boss" told Hugo to take Edward door to door while the rest of the group wandered off. Some went in search of food. Others looked for more to steal.

"What are you doing?" Edward asked.

"*We* are going begging," Hugo replied. He was walking in front of Edward. He was tired of this boy and his strange talk.

"Excuse me?" Edward stopped in his tracks. "You may do as you wish, but I will not beg."

Hugo paid no attention to Edward. He had already found their first target. He fell to the ground, moaning and crying. Edward was confused. What on Earth was this boy doing?

Edward looked up to see a man walking toward them. The man stopped when he saw Hugo on the ground. "My goodness, young man," he said. "What is wrong?"

"Oh, sir," Hugo moaned. "My brother and I were on our way home when I became ill."

"Is there anything I can do?" he asked. The man knelt beside Hugo.

"Could you spare a penny for some food?

Even a small morsel will make me feel better, I'm certain."

"One penny?" the man said. "Why, you shall have three!" He took three pennies from his pocket and handed them to Hugo. "Take these and get yourself some bread. Now come here, boy," the man said to Edward. "Help me carry your brother to your house."

"He is not my brother," Edward said. He crossed his arms over his chest.

"What? Not your brother?"

"He is a beggar and a thief," Edward said.

"You are both thieves!" the man said. He stood up. "Police!" he called. "Someone call the police. These two boys were trying to trick me! One of them played sick so the other could rob me. Help!"

Hugo jumped up and ran away. He disappeared around a corner in only a few seconds. Edward took advantage of this moment of freedom. He turned and ran in the other direction. He knew that the police would not believe him.

Edward ran out of the town and back down the road. He ran for as long as he could. Luckily, he came to a farmhouse not far from town. He thought about knocking on the door, but he felt too tired. Edward did not want to risk more laughter or insults. He was tired of telling the truth only to have no one believe him. Only Miles was on his side, and Edward had no idea how to find him.

Edward walked toward the barn. He looked around to make sure no one was there. It was perfectly quiet. Edward went inside and found a place to lie down. It felt nice and warm.

Just as Edward was about to fall asleep, he sensed something nearby. It was large and had a strange smell. Edward lay perfectly still. He was terrified that this thing might notice him. He stretched his hand out gently, but he was too frightened and quickly pulled it back. He tried again, then again. Finally, he reached just far enough to touch a rope. He turned to look and realized that it wasn't a rope at all! It was a calf's tail.

Edward was relieved to know that this strange creature was only a calf. He was also happy to know that he was not alone. He felt so lonely and friendless. It was nice to have a companion. Edward curled into the calf and fell asleep stroking the animal's neck.

CHAPTER 12

A Time of Sharing

Edward opened his eyes the next morning to see two children staring at him. A boy and a girl stood watching him in silence. Edward stared right back at them.

"Who are you?" the girl asked.

"I am the future king," Edward said.

"The future king?" the boy asked. "King of what?"

"The king of England," Edward replied.

The children looked at each other in

amazement. "Can—can he be telling the truth?" the girl whispered.

"Well," the boy said thoughtfully, "I've never seen the future king, so I can't say that he isn't."

"If you truly are the future king," he added, "then we'll believe you."

"I truly am," Edward replied. He smiled. At long last someone believed him.

"Then you should come inside," the girl said. "Our mother is just making breakfast. You can join us."

Edward followed the children into the house. Their mother welcomed him warmly. She noticed the state of his clothes and the dirt on his face. Her children told her that he was the future king of England. She watched him sit at her table and eat a bowl of oatmeal. He certainly was proper and polite. She felt pity for this poor boy.

"We're happy to have you here, Your Majesty,"

she said. "It is an honor to have you at our table."

Edward finished his breakfast. He sat back in his chair, full and satisfied. The woman and her children were getting ready to go out to work. As she walked out the door, she asked Edward to clean up the breakfast dishes.

What? he thought. *The future king of England washing dishes?* He almost protested, but then he thought again. *I should repay her kindness with a bit of kindness. It's the least I can do.*

He did not do a very good job. He was surprised at how hard it was to clean the wooden spoons and bowls. It took him a very long time. It was far from a perfect job, but Edward was proud of himself. He had learned to do something completely new.

Edward continued to help the widow throughout the morning. He peeled some apples—very poorly—and swept the floor—just as poorly.

Just before noon, the widow sent him out to the barn with her son to help feed the cows. Edward did as she asked.

He followed the younger boy's instructions and poured grain into the trough for the cows. He was not used to this difficult work. The boy noticed that Edward was struggling with the bag of grain. "Can I get you a cup of water?" he asked. "You look very thirsty."

"Yes, please," Edward said. "That is very kind of you." The younger boy ran back to the house while Edward continued his work.

Suddenly Edward heard a familiar voice behind him and dropped the bag of grain.

"Have you given up your princely ways?" Mr. Canty asked.

Edward turned around slowly. Mr. Canty stood with his hands on his hips. He smiled meanly at Edward.

The boy thought about running, but he was

trapped. He knew he had no hope of escape. Hugo approached the barn door. He was surprised to see Edward inside. He and Mr. Canty had stumbled upon the barn when they were looking for shelter. They certainly hadn't expected to find the boy here. Without a word, Mr. Canty grabbed Edward's arm while Hugo put a hand over the boy's mouth. They moved so quickly and quietly that no one in the house heard a thing.

CHAPTER 13

Back Among the Thieves

～∞

King Foo Foo was traveling with the group of
thieves again. Mr. Canty picked on Edward whenever the "Boss" turned his back. Hugo stepped on
his toes. He bumped into Edward and pretended
it was an accident. He even tried to trip Edward.

Edward refused to take any of Hugo's taunts.
He would not sink to Hugo's level. He also refused
to participate in any of the group's illegal activi-
ties. Edward would not steal with them. He
would not beg in the streets. He walked with
them and waited for a chance to escape.

Hugo was working on a plan of his own. He realized that the only way to get rid of Edward was to have him arrested. If Edward escaped, then Mr. Canty would search for him. But if he was in jail, they could go on without him. Hugo was tired of this boy taking up everyone's attention. He had come to think of Mr. Canty as his own father and did not want the competition.

Hugo offered to take Edward into the next village to look for money. He looked for the right target very carefully. He knew he had only one chance. Then he spotted a woman carrying a basket of food. Hugo moved very quickly. He grabbed the basket from the woman and ran off.

Edward could not believe his luck. He was alone! He was just about to turn and run the other way when Hugo appeared again. He thrust the basket into Edward's arms. Before Edward had a chance to realize what had happened, Hugo shouted, "Stop! Thief!" Then he ran around a corner so he could watch the action from afar.

Edward dropped the basket. The woman rushed up to him and grabbed her food. Several people came with her. They took ahold of Edward.

"Let me go!" Edward called. "I have done nothing wrong."

The crowd grew, and more people closed in around Edward. The boy was close to giving up when he heard a familiar voice. "Step away from the boy!"

Edward watched as a long sword parted the crowd. Everyone stepped aside and Miles walked toward the future king.

"Sir Miles," Edward said. "I've been wondering when you would arrive."

Miles leaned in to whisper in Edward's ear. "We must be careful, Sir. There are still many more of them than us." He smiled. He had forgotten that he was now Sir Miles. The boy's memory was still very strong, despite his madness. Miles was impressed.

Just then a policeman arrived. Before the policeman had a chance to speak, Miles said, "Thank goodness you've arrived. Please lead the way, and we'll follow you." Miles put his hand on Edward's shoulder and told him to stay quiet. The future king obeyed.

As they followed the policeman, Miles and Edward spoke quietly to each other.

"Laws are made by the king, correct?" Miles asked. Edward nodded. "How can we respect and resist them at the same time? We must have faith that these laws will protect the innocent just as they punish the guilty."

Edward hoped that Miles was right. He had

seen an awful lot over the past few days that caused him to wonder.

Edward went before the judge, and the woman with the basket entered the court. The judge asked the woman to reveal the contents of the basket. It was a plump pig ready for cooking.

"What do you guess this pig is worth?" the judge asked.

"Three shillings and eight pence, sir," she replied.

The judge looked around his crowded court-room. He asked the guards to remove everyone but Miles, Edward, and the woman.

"Madam," the judge said. "Please consider this matter fully. This boy was quite likely hungry and tired when he stole your basket. Having no food will make us do strange things. Now Madam, do you realize that anyone who steals something worth more than two shillings and four pence will be sent to a workhouse?"

Edward gasped. He had no idea such a thing was possible. He knew this was a serious matter, but was it possible that he could go to a work-house?

"Oh heavens, no!" the woman cried. "What have I done? This boy cannot go to a workhouse because of me. What should I do?"

"My advice is to lower the value of the pig," the judge said calmly.

"Then call the pig eight pence," she said.

Miles was so excited that he hugged Edward in front of everyone. The boy was embarrassed, but he said nothing.

The woman picked up her basket and quickly left the courtroom. One of the guards held the door for her, then followed her out. Miles, curious to know why the guard left, followed them outside.

"That is a fat pig," the guard said to the woman. "I'll buy it from you. Here is your eight pence."

"Eight pence!" the woman laughed. "Don't be ridiculous! This pig is worth much more than that."

"Ah, but Madam, you swore under oath that this pig was worth eight pence. Were you lying?" The guard smiled. He considered himself very clever. Seeing no way out of her situation, the woman gave her pig to the guard. He took the pig and hid it in a secret spot before returning to the court.

Miles went back to Edward just in time to hear him sentenced to a short time in jail. The boy was furious. He was about to rant and yell when Miles once again put his hand on his shoulder. "I ask you to be patient for only a bit longer, Sir. I promise that you won't suffer any time in jail."

Edward decided to trust Miles and stay quiet. After all, what other choice did he have?

Miles and Edward followed the guard through a public square. The sun was setting and the air was getting cooler. People were heading back to their homes to stay warm.

Miles tapped the guard on the shoulder. "I would like to speak with you for a moment," Miles said.

"We have no time for that," the guard replied. "The boy is expected at the jail."

"I'll say this to you once and I hope you understand," Miles said. He leaned close to the guard. "Let the boy escape."

"What? That's ridiculous!"

"I heard every word you said to that woman. Would you like me to report it to the judge?" Miles spoke quietly. "You will certainly lose your job if the judge learns you cheated that honest woman." He paused for a moment. "Or, perhaps the judge will decide that *you* deserve time in jail."

The guard stared at Miles in disbelief. He couldn't speak.

"Very well, then," Miles said. "I will run back to the court to have a word with the judge." He turned to leave, but the guard grabbed his arm.

"No, wait. The judge will have no sympathy for me." The guard took a deep breath. "Very well, then. It seems that I have no choice. Be quick about it, though." The guard took another deep breath and turned his back.

"I'll count to ten," he said. "If you're still there when I turn back around, I'll take you both to jail."

Miles and Edward were far away and down many streets before the guard even counted to eight.

CHAPTER 14

Hendon Hall

◌∽

The journey to Hendon Hall took several days on horseback. Finally Miles said, "Look, Sir." He pointed to a large house on a hill. "There is my home! Hendon Hall." Edward noticed that Miles had tears in his eyes.

"I wonder if anyone will remember me," he said. "Will all the same servants still be there? No, I'm being silly." Miles shook his head slightly. "My father, brothers, and Lady Edith will be mad with joy to see me." He looked to Edward. "And, they will be quite pleased to meet you."

Miles stepped off his horse. He walked up to the house and burst through the front door. Edward was close behind him.

Inside, the house looked gray and solemn. The rooms felt cold despite large fires in the hearths. Miles walked briskly into the front room. A man was sitting in front of the fire. His back was to the door.

"Hugh!" Miles called. "How good to see you. Stand up and give your brother a hug."

Hugh stood up quickly. When he saw Miles, he jumped back. At first he looked surprised, but he soon regained his sense of calm. He looked closely at Miles.

"I'm afraid, stranger, that you are confused. I am not your brother." Hugh frowned at Miles. He had recognized his brother instantly, but he didn't want Miles to know that.

"Pardon me," Miles said. He took another step forward. "Aren't you Hugh Hendon?"

"Yes, I am Hugh," he said. "It is you that I have my doubts about."

"I'm Miles! I know that I've been away a long time, but I can't have changed that much."

"How dare you!" Hugh stood up straight. "My brother died seven years ago. Remove yourself this instant, or I will have you arrested as a fraud."

Miles tried to protest, but Hugh held his hand up.

"We received a letter saying that my brother Miles was killed in battle. We mourned his loss many years ago."

"Bring me to our father," Miles said. He was almost shouting. Why wouldn't his brother believe him? "Our father will recognize me instantly."

"One cannot call the dead," Hugh said calmly.

"Our father has died?" Miles held his head in

his hands. "Our poor sweet father." He looked back at Hugh. "And what of the Lady Edith? Is she well? Does she still live in Hendon Hall?"

"Of course," Hugh said.

"And our brother, Arthur?" Miles asked. "Does he still live?"

"No," Hugh said. "*My* brother died some six years ago."

"Then bring in the servants. They will recognize me. Someone from my youth will know me. They have all worked here for many years."

"Alas, almost all are gone," Hugh said. "But I will bring some in if that will prove your point." Hugh left the room.

Miles paced back and forth. "I don't understand any of this," he said. "After so many years in a prison camp—my escape—my troubles in returning home—and now no one recognizes me. It is like a bad dream." He turned to Edward.

"Please believe me, Your Majesty. This is my home. That was my brother Hugh. My name is Miles Hendon."

"I do not doubt you," Edward said simply. "You did not doubt me. I will give you the same respect."

Once again tears came to Miles' eyes. "Thank you, Sir," he said. "I thank you with all my heart."

Suddenly, a door opened. A beautiful woman entered followed closely by Hugh. She walked slowly. Her head was lowered, and her eyes were fixed on the floor. She looked horribly sad.

"Edith!" Miles called. "My darling."

Edward noticed that the woman trembled slightly when Miles spoke. She began to blush.

Hugh held up his hand and stepped between them. He turned to Edith. "Look at this man. Do you know him?"

She paused for a few seconds before looking up. "I do not know him," she said quickly. She returned her gaze to the floor. A moment later she ran from the room, fighting back tears.

Miles sank into a chair. He held his head and moaned.

Servants entered the room, and Hugh asked if they recognized Miles. They all shook their heads in silence.

"So there you have it," Hugh said. "There must be some mistake. The servants don't recognize you. My wife does not recognize you…"

"Your wife?" Miles looked up at Hugh. In an instant, Hugh was pinned against the wall. "Now I know what you've done. You wrote that letter yourself. You convinced everyone that I was dead and took my place. Why else would Edith marry you? You wanted her money so you faked my death. You took my love!"

Hugh called to the servants to help.

"But sir," one of them said, "he is armed."

"Are you all cowards?" Hugh screamed.

"They can do as they like," Miles said. "I have only one thing to say. I, Miles Hendon, am master of Hendon Hall, and I will not leave. Do not doubt me!"

Hugh signaled again for the servants. They pulled Miles away from their master. Hugh sneered at Miles before storming out of the room.

CHAPTER 15

Miles the Impostor

Edward and Miles sat in the front room of Hendon Hall thinking about their next move. Or rather, Miles was thinking about what to do next. Edward was beginning to wonder why no one was searching for him.

"They must have realized by now that a fraud is living in the palace," Edward said. "Why has no one come for me?"

There was a light tap on the door, and Edith entered the room. Miles sprang forward to greet her, but she held her hand up slightly. Miles stopped in his tracks. She was still beautiful but very sad.

"I have come to warn you," she said. Her voice was quiet and she turned to look behind her several times. "My husband is master of this region. He has power over everything and everyone." She paused for a moment. "He always gets his way."

Miles ignored her comments. "Don't you recognize me, Edith? Don't you see that I am Miles?"

She swallowed and took a deep breath. She could not look him in the eye. "I can only warn you. You must escape. You must leave now."

"I will not leave my home again," Miles said firmly.

"Don't you understand?" Her cheeks were red and she was breathing heavily. "This is not your home anymore. My husband is a tyrant. You are not safe here." She turned to look behind her again. "None of us are truly safe here."

"You ask me to leave after saying something like that? Are you worried that he will hurt you?" Miles moved closer, but she stopped him again with a wave of her hand.

"Please take this money. It will help you on your travels." She held a purse toward him.

"Do one favor for me," Miles said. "Look me in the eye just once. Look me in the eye, and say you do not recognize me."

At that moment, the door burst open. Several servants rushed into the room and grabbed the two visitors. After a terrible struggle, Miles was overpowered. He and Edward were dragged away and thrown into prison.

CHAPTER 16

Prison

∽

The prison cell was crowded and terribly dirty. Men and women were both trapped inside the tiny space. Some were handcuffed to a wall. Others were chained to beds. No one had much room to move around.

When they had first arrived, Miles had been overcome with rage and grief. He could not think straight. He was focused on his brother's crimes and could think of nothing else. After some time, though, Miles began to calm down. He tried to figure out whether Edith had recognized him, but he could make no sense of it. His homecoming had been such a surprising and disappointing experience.

A few days passed while Miles and Edward wasted away in the prison cell. They suffered through the dirty conditions and poor food. Edward was no longer claiming to be king. Things was already difficult enough with everyone calling Miles a fake.

Miles was quite famous in the jail. Guards would often stop by to insult him. They occasionally brought people by who might recognize him, but no one said they knew him. Then one day they brought by an old man. He was another prisoner—one of the old servants from Hendon Hall. The guards pointed to Miles and asked "Is that your old master?"

The old man looked at Miles and shook his head. "I've no idea who you're talking about," he said. "I've never seen that man before."

The guards laughed again and left the old man with Miles. When they were safely out of ear shot, the old man whispered, "Thank goodness!" and smiled. "At long last my master has returned. We thought you were dead all these years."

"George?" Miles said. "Is that you? What are you doing here?"

"The same thing as you. Your brother threw a lot of us in here. If it weren't for all the dirt and grub, you might recognize more of us."

And so Miles learned the story of his family. As Hugh had told them, Arthur had died six years earlier. The stress of Arthur's death and Miles's disappearance caused Sir Richard to become sick. Sir Richard wanted Hugh and Edith to be safe and married, but Edith begged for more time. She was certain Miles would return or send word. Sir Richard agreed. Then one day a letter arrived saying that Miles had been killed in battle. Sir Richard felt there was no point in waiting any longer, and Hugh and Edith were married. It was not long before talk spread through the countryside that Edith had found several drafts of the letter announcing Miles's death in her husband's own handwriting. But she had no hope of divorce. She had no other family and no means of support. If she left, Hugh would take all of her money and Edith would have nothing. When Sir Richard died, Hugh took over the family fortune as well. He was not well liked. In fact, most people feared him. Everyone knew that he was quick to throw people into jail. No one felt safe standing up to him.

"That is an awful tale, George," Miles said. I would do anything to change it."

"It is a strange time for everyone," George replied. "I have heard other rumors that the young, future king is mad. I hear they are keeping him away from the public."

Suddenly Edward spoke up. "The future king

is not mad!" he said. "You will do everyone some good if you stick to your own matters."

The old servant shrugged his shoulders and returned to his own thoughts.

"The old king will be buried in a day or two," George said. "The new king will be crowned a few days after that. I do wish I could take part in the celebrations. You miss so much when you're in prison."

Edward sat in a state of shock. Was that little peasant boy still in the palace? For the first time, Edward realized that someone else might be crowned in his place.

When their prison term finally ended, Miles and Edward headed back down the road. Miles was quite sad. He knew he could not go home. Hugh would simply have him jailed as a fraud again. All that he had hoped for was gone. Everyone whom he loved was gone. He wondered if he had lost his energy to fight, too.

Edward, on the other hand, had a new strength. He marched down the road with determination. Miles caught sight of him and, for a moment, forgot his own problems. He found himself cheering up.

"I have not asked you," Miles said, "where are we going?"

"To London, of course."

When Miles and Edward arrived in the city a few days later, they discovered that they were just in time. King Henry had been buried, and Tom was to be crowned king the next day.

CHAPTER 17

Coronation Day

⎍⎍

Life in the palace was sad for Tom. The kingdom was still mourning King Henry, and Elizabeth and Jane's sorrow made Tom upset as well. But in spite of this, Tom was learning to enjoy his life as the future king. He could read books whenever he wanted. He could demand that Elizabeth or Jane come see him whenever he wanted. He could eat all the food he desired. He was even enjoying the ritual of getting dressed and undressed. He loved

his expensive clothes and ordered more. He was especially fond of hearing the call, "Make way for the king," whenever he walked into a room.

Did Tom Canty ever think of the rightful prince? The boy who was still lost in the world somewhere? For the first few days, he was racked with guilt and worry. However, those feelings soon faded away. His concern about his mother and sisters faded away, too. When he did think of them—their dirty rags and messy hair—he felt a shudder. Eventually, he barely thought of them at all.

On the morning of the coronation, Tom awoke to music. This music was entirely for him. This was the day he was to be crowned king. The entire country was rejoicing. Tom felt very happy indeed.

When Tom arrived at the church, he was led to the front of it. He looked at the people gathered around him. They were all happy and excited. They cheered his arrival and called for "King Edward." Tom's heart swelled with pride. He felt there was nothing more important than becoming king of England.

Suddenly Tom saw his mother. He was shocked. He threw his hand in front of his face, palm facing outward, to block his view. It was the gesture his mother remembered. She knew instantly that this was her son!

She pushed her way to the front of the crowd and grabbed his arm. She began to cry. "Oh, my child," she wailed. "Thank goodness you are safe! I have prayed for you every night and every morning." She looked up at him, her face filled with joy.

Tom was just about to say, "I do not know you," when a guard pulled her from Tom. The guard threw her to the ground with a stern warning. When Tom saw his mother fall, his heart nearly broke. All of his pride quickly washed away. For the first time in weeks, Tom did not want to be king.

The crowd continued to call for King Edward, but Tom could not hear them. He felt trapped again. The only thing he could hear was his own voice. The words "I do not know you," repeated over and over in his head.

Lord Hertford noticed Tom's downcast eyes and sad look. "Your Majesty," he whispered. "People will notice that you are unhappy. That will not do today. You must rejoice so they may rejoice."

Tom looked at Hertford. He was afraid he might start to cry. "But, that woman," he said quietly, "is my mother."

Lord Hertford gasped. The king had gone mad again! They all thought the boy was recovering. It must be the excitement of the day. *We must keep him close to us*, Hertford thought, *in case he says too much.*

Hertford led Tom to the throne. The throne sat on a special stage so everyone in the church could see him. Tom sat down very slowly. He looked around him. The crowd was quiet as they waited for the crown to be placed on his head. The only sound Tom could hear was his own breath. It was very loud.

The Archbishop of Canterbury picked up the royal crown and walked over to Tom. He held the crown above the boy's head and said a short prayer. Just as the Archbishop was about to lower the crown, a voice called out:

"I forbid you to set the crown of England upon that impostor's head. I am the true king!"

A group of guards immediately surrounded Edward. They were trying to drag him from the church when they heard another voice.

"Stop!" Tom called. "Let him go. He is the king!"

The crowd began to mumble and stir. What on Earth was going on? No one had ever seen anything like it.

Hertford stepped to the front of the altar. "Do not panic!" he called out. "His Majesty is merely having one of his spells. Pay him no mind." Hertford pointed to Edward, who was still surrounded by guards. "Take this beggar out of here this instant."

"Do not touch him," Tom said. "On my command, I say let him go." The guards let go of Edward. "I tell you, he is the true king of England."

Edward walked to altar and climbed the steps. Tom ran to meet him. He gave the boy a big hug.

"I am so glad you have finally returned," he said. Tom was surprised at how relieved he felt now that the game was over.

Everyone in the room gasped when the two boys stood side-by-side. They were identical. Could it be true that the king of England was living as a pauper? Had they almost crowned a pauper as the king of England?

"This is very confusing," Hertford said. "I'm not sure what to do."

"Ask me a question," Edward said. "Ask me anything to do with the court."

So Hertford and some of the other lords asked Edward questions. He answered them all correctly. Tom was feeling excited. It looked like he would soon be able to go home.

At last Hertford said, "It is very impressive, I'll admit. However, our young king could do the same. This is not proof that the beggar is the king."

The Lord Protector stepped forward. "I have a question," he said. "If you are the true king, you will know the answer to it. Where is the royal seal? It has been lost for several days now."

Edward looked stunned. He could not remember the last place he had seen the royal seal.

Tom, noticing his confusion, tried to help him along. "Please, Your Majesty, think hard. I'm sure it will come to you. What did you do on your last day in the palace?"

Edward looked at Tom. He appreciated this boy's help. Perhaps he was not as bad as he thought. "Well, I was working with Lord Hertford in my room. We had the royal seal then!" Edward looked pleased with himself. "I left my work on the desk and went outside to exercise in the yard. That's when I saw you at the gate." Edward nodded to Tom.

"We went back to my room for something to eat. We changed our clothes. Then I ran outside to talk to the guards…" Edward paused for a moment. "Wait!" he cried. "I remember now. Before I left the room, I hid the work and the royal seal." Edward told the Lord Protector to look in a secret drawer at the back of his desk. He would find the royal seal stored there.

Everyone in the church waited quietly while the Lord Protector and some guards searched the desk. Tom and Edward stared at each other with wide eyes. Neither could believe that this strange

time was almost over. They both said silent prayers that the royal seal would be found.

The Lord Protector ran back into the church. He held the royal seal high in the air. Everyone began to cheer.

"Long live the true king! Long live the true King Edward!"

Tom stepped away from the throne. He took his robe off and held it out for Edward.

The Lord Protector pointed to Tom. "Guards! Take this fraud to prison!"

"No!" Edward said firmly. "If it weren't for him, I would not have my crown again. No one shall harm this boy. He is a true friend."

CHAPTER 18

A Happy Ending at Last!

∽

While all the excitement was going on inside the church, poor Miles was trapped outside. He had lost Edward in the crowd earlier that morning. He decided to wait until the crowd left so he could search more easily. He knew that Edward would be somewhere nearby.

It was already late afternoon by the time Miles saw the king. He could not believe his eyes. It was his pauper! Was that possible? Miles looked at the group beside the king and noticed another boy.

But wait, was this boy his pauper? The two boys were nearly identical.

Miles walked toward them in a daze. He did not hear the guards call him. He was too focused on this mystery. He only stopped when a guard stood in front of him.

"Stand back," the guard said.

King Edward looked over when he heard the guard speak. "Let him come to me," he said. "Sir Miles has every right to be here."

"Y-your Majesty," Miles stuttered. "You've found your crown."

Edward smiled. "Yes. Thanks to you and your bravery."

"I'm sorry, Sir," Miles said. "I think I'm still in a bit of shock."

"That's quite understandable," Edward replied. "Now that I have returned home and learned of all of Tom's troubles convincing people of the truth, I realize that my story must have seemed unbelievable. I've been waiting for you to arrive. I have a present for you." Edward looked to the group of people standing nearby.

"Sir Hugh!" he called. "Come to me."

Miles's brother Hugh quickly walked to the king and knelt before him. "Yes, Your Majesty," he said.

"Sir Hugh, I would like you to look at this man. Do you recognize him?"

Hugh turned around. He gasped when he saw Miles. "I—no, Sir. This man is a fraud! I swear."

"I know all about your crimes," Edward said. "I know that you stole your brother's rightful property. Guards! Take this man to prison."

Hugh cried out as they dragged him away.

Not long after, there was yet another happy reunion as Tom rushed into his mother's arms. He had so many stories to tell her. And there was the happy news that the new king had given them a new home. They would have clean clothes and honest work. Mrs. Canty, Nan, and Bet laughed.

"I always knew you were destined for great things," Mrs. Canty said.

"It was very kind of King Edward to help us," Bet said.

"Yes, he's very generous," Nan added.

Tom smiled at his family. "It's true," he said. "There is no one as kind and generous as our good King Edward."

And so we come to the end of our tale. Hugh did not stay in jail for long. Miles and Edith did not want him to suffer too much. When he was released, Hugh decided to leave England and set out for America. Edith divorced Hugh, and Miles and Edith were married shortly after he left.

The Cantys lived a happy and contented life in their new home. Their grandmother passed away one night in her sleep, and Mr. Canty never reappeared. Everything was quiet and comfortable for the rest of their days.

What Do *You* Think?
Questions for Discussion

⌒

Have you ever been around a toddler who keeps asking the question "Why?" Does your teacher call on you in class with questions from your homework? Do your parents ask you questions about your day at the dinner table? We are always surrounded by questions that need a specific response. But is it possible to have a question with no right answer?

The following questions are about the book you just read. But this is not a quiz! They are designed to help you look at the people, places, and events in the story from different angles.

These questions do not have specific answers. Instead, they might make you think of the story in a completely new way.

Think carefully about each question and enjoy discovering more about this classic story.

1. On his way to the castle, Tom realizes that he has never been so far from home before. How do you think this makes him feel? What is the farthest you've ever been from home?

2. Who is the Prince of Poverty and who is the Prince of Plenty? Do you know anyone like either of the boys? Which of them are you more like?

3. When Edward and Tom switch lives, they find out that it is not all they hoped for. Which of the boys do you think had a harder time adjusting to his new life? Have you ever wanted to live someone else's life?

4. When he is mistaken for Edward, Tom begins to fantasize about what he would do if he

was actually the king. Why does he stop thinking about this? What would you do if you were king or queen?

5. The two boys think of school very differently. Tom enjoys learning, while Edward considers his lessons a burden. How do you feel about school? What is your favorite subject?

6. Why does Miles choose to help Edward? Have you ever helped a stranger? What did you do?

7. Tom says that he feels horribly lonely, yet he is never alone. What do you think he means by this? Have you ever felt the same way?

8. When Edward learns that he is the king, he says, "I am now King Edward. Isn't it strange that no one can see me?" What does he mean by this? Have you ever felt invisible?

9. Why do you think Edward is willing to help the widow with the household chores? Do you have chores?

10. When Miles returns home, his brother says, "I'm afraid, stranger, that you are confused. I am not your brother." How do you suppose this makes Miles feel? Do you have any siblings? Do you get along with them?

Afterword

by Arthur Pober, Ed.D.

༄

First impressions are important.

Whether we are meeting new people, going to new places, or picking up a book unknown to us, first impressions count for a lot. They can lead to warm, lasting memories or can make us shy away from any future encounters.

Can you recall your own first impressions and earliest memories of reading the classics?

Do you remember wading through pages and pages of text to prepare for an exam? Or were you the child who hid under the blanket to read with a flashlight, joining forces with Robin Hood to save Maid Marian? Do you remember only how long it took you to read a lengthy novel such as Little Women? Or did you become best friends with the March sisters?

Even for a gifted young reader, getting through long chapters with dense language can easily become overwhelming and can obscure the richness of the story and its characters. Reading an abridged, newly crafted version of a classic novel can be the gentle introduction a child needs to explore the characters and storyline without the frustration of difficult vocabulary and complex themes.

Reading an abridged version of a classic novel gives the young reader a sense of independence and the satisfaction of finishing a "grown-up" book. And when a child is engaged with and inspired by a classic story, the tone is set for further exploration of the story's themes, characters, history, and details. As a child's reading skills advance, the desire to tackle the original, unabridged version of the story will naturally emerge.

If made accessible to young readers, these stories can become invaluable tools for understanding themselves in the context of their families and social environments. This is why the Classic Starts series includes questions that stimulate discussion regarding the impact and social relevance of the characters and stories today. These questions can foster lively conversations between children and their parents or teachers. When we look at the issues, values, and standards of past times in terms of how we live now, we can appreciate literature's classic tales in a very personal and engaging way.

Share your love of reading the classics with a young child, and introduce an imaginary world real enough to last a lifetime.

Dr. Arthur Pober, Ed.D.

Dr. Arthur Pober has spent more than twenty years in the fields of early childhood and gifted education. He is the former principal of one of the world's oldest laboratory schools for gifted youngsters, Hunter College Elementary School, and former Director of Magnet Schools for the Gifted and Talented for more than 25,000 youngsters in New York City.

Dr. Pober is a recognized authority in the areas of media and child protection and is currently the U.S. representative to the European Institute for the Media and European Advertising Standards Alliance.

Explore these wonderful stories in our
Classic Starts™ library.

20,000 Leagues Under the Sea

The Adventures of Huckleberry Finn

The Adventures of Robin Hood

The Adventures of Sherlock Holmes

The Adventures of Tom Sawyer

Anne of Green Gables

Around the World in 80 Days

Black Beauty

The Call of the Wild

Dracula

Frankenstein

Gulliver's Travels

Heidi

A Little Princess

Little Women

Oliver Twist

Pollyanna

The Prince and the Pauper

Rebecca of Sunnybrook Farm

The Red Badge of Courage

Robinson Crusoe

The Secret Garden

The Story of King Arthur and His Knights

The Strange Case of Dr. Jekyll and Mr. Hyde

The Swiss Family Robinson

The Three Musketeers

Treasure Island

The War of the Worlds

White Fang

The Wind in the Willows